The Pirates of the Spanish Main

Douglas Botting

With illustrations by Gareth Floyd

Explorer 9

Puffin Books

Puffin Books: a Division of Penguin Books Ltd, Harmondsworth, Middlesex, England
Penguin Books Inc., 7110 Ambassador Road, Baltimore, Maryland 21207, U.S.A.
Penguin Books Australia Ltd, Ringwood, Victoria, Australia

First published 1973

Made and printed in Great Britain by
W. S. Cowell Ltd, Butter Market, Ipswich

Acknowledgements. The publishers and the author would like to thank the
following for their kind permission to reproduce the photographs
appearing in this book:

The Trustees of the British Museum, pp. 6, 14, 18, 21, 23 and 43;
Lutterworth Press, pp. 4 and 47; The Mansell Collection, p. 46; The
National Maritime Museum, London, pp. 8-9; Pelham Books, p. 34.

Tom. 1. pag. 11.

One of the original boucaniers (buccaneers).

The story of the pirates of the Spanish Main is a true story. These strange, wild, bad-tempered men – the villains of *Treasure Island* and other tales – really did live once, really did walk planks, cut throats, drink rum, wear peg legs, fight duels and bury treasure. Who were they? Why did they become what they were? How did they?

It all began when the first Spaniards under the command of Christopher Columbus arrived in the New World in 1492 and laid claim to it in the name of the king of Spain. Within fifty years the Spaniards had created the largest empire on earth, stretching from California to Cape Horn and from the Atlantic to the Pacific. This empire included the southern regions of what is now the United States, all the West Indian islands, and all of Central and South America, except Brazil, which had been claimed by Portugal under the Treaty of Tordesillas of 1494. According to the treaty, Spain had the right to all of the regions lying west of a line running from pole to pole 370 leagues west of the Cape Verde Islands, while Portugal had the right to all the regions lying east of the line.

The Spanish possessions in the New World – a vast territory of steaming jungles, snowy mountains and endless plains – were fabulously fertile and rich. Vast quantities of gold, silver and precious stones were produced from the mines of Mexico and Peru, and these were shipped each year to Spain in special convoys of galleons. The Spanish were very jealous of their American possessions and all the riches they found in them. Not only did they proclaim absolute rule over them but they prevented any foreigners from coming near them, either to trade or to settle. In effect they were keeping everybody else out of what amounted to half the known land on earth. All the wealth of the New World had to go to Spain and nowhere else. All the goods that went into the New World had to come from Spain and nowhere else.

The other nations of Europe – especially England, France and Holland – resented this. Since it was impossible to trade peacefully with the Spanish, the only way for them to share in the riches of the Americas was to steal them. So, in the last half of the sixteenth century, English sea captains like Drake, Hawkins and Oxenham began a series of spectacular raids on the Spanish Main, which was the name they gave to the tropical Caribbean shore of Spanish America. There they attacked the Spanish treasure trains on land, captured the Spanish treasure ships at sea, and came home with fortunes.

The power of Spain was in decline by this time, and early in the seventeenth century immigrants from various European countries were able to settle on some of the small Caribbean islands that were not inhabited by Spaniards. One

of these islands was called Tortuga, off the northern coast of Haiti. About the year 1630 this little place was occupied by a band of wild French adventurers called *boucaniers*. Previously the *boucaniers* had earned their living by hunting and selling strips of dried meat which they smoked in small beehive-shaped huts called *boucanes*, from which they derived their name. But they soon found there was more money to be made from hunting at sea than from hunting on land, and before long the *boucaniers* (or buccaneers as they were called in English) had turned seamen and were busy raiding the Spanish Main.

Naturally the Spanish called them pirates. But true pirates were the enemies of all mankind and attacked ships of every nationality. The buccaneers, on the other hand, attacked nobody but the Spanish. They preferred to be called privateers – that is private warships in the legitimate service of their government and certified by a special commission or letter of marque. From time to time they were also called sea-rovers, freebooters and corsairs.

Eventually, as the English, French and Dutch established more and more colonies in the West Indies, the ranks of the buccaneers were swelled by the outcasts of many nations – deserters, deportees, political and religious refugees, down-and-outs. To such landless, lawless, and penniless men the buccaneering life had obvious attractions. You had a chance to make easy money. You were your own boss. You had an interesting time.

But they were terrible men, some of those early buccaneers. Men like Rock Braziliano, who was hairy like an ape, or L'Ollonois, who drank blood, were really mentally disturbed. The Frenchman L'Ollonois, for instance, never thought twice about slaughtering a dozen Spanish prisoners at a time in cold blood. Once, during a raid on Nicaragua, he cut out a prisoner's heart and began to eat it. 'I'll do the same to you, if you don't look out,' he told the others. Eventually even his own shipmates couldn't put up with him any more and marooned him among the Indians. The Indians didn't care for him either and tore him to pieces limb by limb and burnt the bits to ashes.

5

The pirate fort on Tortuga.

Rock Braziliano and Frederick L'Ollonois – two of the fiercest pirates who ever sailed the Spanish Main.

The Brotherhood of the Coast, as the international body of buccaneers was called, was very well organized. The men were rough and tough but on active service they kept good discipline and were generally very fair to one another. Ships captains were elected. If a crew didn't like their captain they could maroon him or change ships. All loot was shared out according to an agreed scale. A captain got two-and-a-half shares, and the first mate, surgeon and shipwright each got one-and-a-half. If there was no loot after a cruise, then nobody got anything – 'no prey, no pay' was the rule.

They even worked out a simple insurance scheme. If you lost your right arm you were awarded 600 pieces of eight or six slaves. For the loss of your left arm you got 500 pieces of eight, for an eye or a finger 100 pieces. Punishments were severe, but fair for those days. For example, anyone who endangered the ship by carrying a lighted candle without a lanthorn in the hold was sentenced to what they called Moses Law, or forty lashes.

The ships they sailed in were usually ones they had captured from the Spanish and were therefore of all sizes and rigs, ranging from little unarmed ten-ton sloops or single-masted, lateen-rigged barques with crews of twenty, to two-masted brigantines and 120-ton flagships carrying maybe fifty guns and 300 men. Most of the ships were very crowded and uncomfortable, with little protection against sun and rain, and often short of provisions.

The buccaneers were superb sailors at sea and first-class guerilla fighters on land. Often they started in a very small way, taking to sea in a dug-out canoe to attack a small coaster, and then using the coaster to attack a bigger prize like an ocean-going galleon carrying gold and silver to Spain.

The buccaneers knew the Caribbean islands and the Spanish Main like the back of their hands. Their favourite haunts were the Yucatan Channel, the Mona Passage, and the jungle-covered creeks and lagoons of the Mosquito Coast. There they would lurk for days until an unsuspecting victim hove into view, then they would give chase, as remorselessly as hunting dogs.

They always kept their bow to the enemy during an attack and cleared the decks with musket fire before boarding – by their reckoning four muskets were the equal of a big cannon.

On sight of an enemy sail, the captain would issue the following orders in readiness for action:

FULL SAILS!
DOWN CHESTS AND UP HAMMOCKS!
SMALL ARMS TO THE QUARTER DECK!
EVERY MAN TO HIS POST!
KNOCK DOWN BULKHEADS AND CABIN PARTITIONS!
CLEAR DECKS FORE AND AFT!
GUNNERS, BEAR OPEN THE PORTHOLES AND OUT WITH THE LOWER TIER!
SOUND DRUMS AND TRUMPETS AND ST GEORGE FOR ENGLAND!
FIRE PROW GUNS!
FIRE BROADSIDE!
LET GO FIREBALLS!
FIRE SMALL SHOT!
FIRE STERN GUNS!

Overleaf: A seventeenth-century map of the Spanish Main, showing where the pirates lived and roamed.

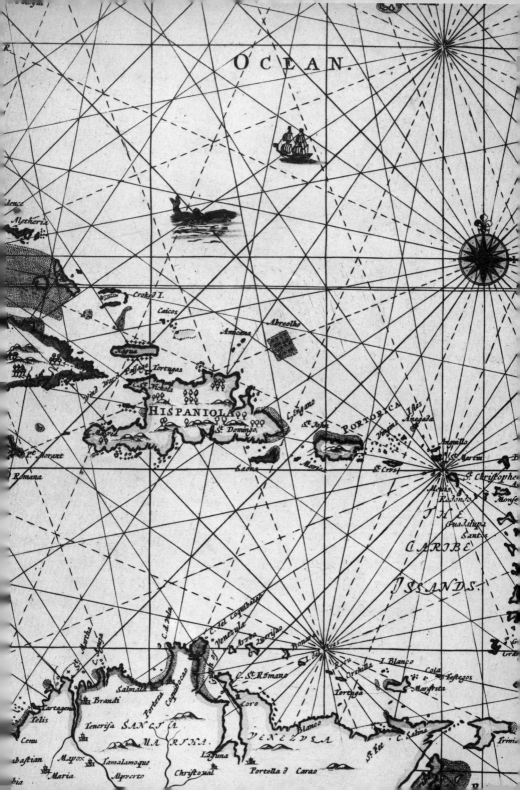

O C E A N.

Crked I.

Caicos

Amcana   Abreotho

Cigna

Tortugas

C: Nichola

HISPANIOLA   Gengmo   St John   PORTORICA   Anegada

St Domingo   Anguillo

                                                     Maria   St Martin

Laena   St Crus   St Christopher

                                                                                   Mevis
                                                                                   Redondo   Monse

                                                                                        Id.
                                                                                   Guadlupa
                                                                                   Santis

                                                                              C A R I B E

                                                                              I S S A N D S.

C: de Coquibacoa
Gulfe of Venezuela   Aruba   Curedipo
                                                                    Bonayre
C. St Romano   I. da   I. Blanco   Cola
                                                         Orchilla   Testigos
                                                    Tortuga   Margarita
Coro
Salmali   Blanco
Tenerifa   S A N C T A   V E N E Z V E L A   C. Salina   Trini
U A   R I K A   St. Ia
Cenu   Mayox   Iamalamoque   Laguna   Portella d Carao
                              Alpverto   Christoval

Depending on how it went the Captain would shout 'What cheer, mates?' and then order the pumps to be manned and the carpenter to go overboard to plug the leaks in the hull. Then the ships would close again. At the end of the day the captain would give the following orders:

SURGEON, LOOK TO THE WOUNDED AND WIND UP THE SLAIN!
SWABBERS, MAKE THE SHIP CLEAN!
PURSER, RECORD THE NAMES OF THE DEAD!
GUNNERS, SPONGE YOUR ORDNANCE!
SOLDIERS, SCOUR YOUR PIECES!
CARPENTER, ABOUT YOUR LEAKS!
BOATSWAIN AND THE REST, REPAIR THE SAILS AND SHROUDS!
COOK, GET READY FOR SUPPER!
BOY, IS THE KETTLE BOILED?
BOATSWAIN, CALL UP THE MEN TO PRAYER!
BOY, FETCH MY CELLAR OF BOTTLES. A HEALTH TO YOU ALL FORE AND AFT!

Sometimes they kept the captured ship after looting it, sometimes they scuttled it by knocking a hole in the bottom – that was usually the cabin boy's job. Sometimes they kept prisoners, sometimes they didn't. Usually the deck of the Spanish ships were swilling in blood by the time the buccaneers broke off the action.

On land the buccaneers' equipment consisted of a very long musket, a bandolier of lead bullets, a powder horn (or a pelican's pouch), four long knives, a mosquito net (to keep off the mosquitoes at night) wrapped round the waist, a sawn-off tricorn hat, old British army cast-off tunics, and boots pulled off the feet of Spanish prisoners. They knew how to survive in difficult country. They were brilliant shots – reputedly they could hit a coin spinning in the air – and they were experts in the use of explosives, fire darts, firewheels, grenades, land mines and devices that burnt under the water.

Their weaknesses were those of all men who earn an irregular wage in a hard and dangerous way. Usually they drank too

The crew of a small pirate ship preparing to board their prize.

much. At sea, off an enemy coast, they sometimes had nothing to drink but brandy captured from Spanish ships, and in hot, thirst-making weather they were drunk for a lot of the time. When they came in port they thought nothing of spending 3,000 pieces of eight[1] in a single night. They chased all the girls, made themselves a nuisance and drank themselves unconscious. This was an easy thing to do in Port Royal, the buccaneer capital.

Port Royal, in Jamaica, used to be considered the wildest city in the world. A London journalist, Ned Ward of *The London Spy*, who visited it in the early 1690s, described it as follows:

The dunghill of the universe, the refuse of all creation, as sickly as a hospital, as dangerous as the plague, as hot as hell and as wicked as the devil. It is subject to tornadoes, hurricanes and earthquakes, as if the island, like the people, were troubled with belly ache.

For all that, Port Royal had an excellent natural harbour and served as the main base for all the biggest buccaneer operations until it met a sudden and terrible end.

[1] A piece of eight was probably worth about 25p at this time, and would probably be worth twenty times more today. But Jamaica was a *very* expensive place.

Overleaf: Victualling a ship at Port Royal.

Henry Morgan – the most successful thief in history.

In 1668 the Governor of Jamaica put a Welshman called Henry Morgan in command of all the buccaneers on the island. Morgan was not a particularly pleasant man but he was an outstanding buccaneer and under his leadership the buccaneers went on to achieve their greatest feat of arms – the capture of the capital of the Spanish American empire itself.

Henry Morgan was born in Glamorgan in 1635. His family were respectable yeomen but he left school too young to receive much education and at the age of eighteen emigrated to Jamaica to seek his fortune. There he soon got caught up in the buccaneering life and on various expeditions against the Spanish he quickly learned all there was to learn about pirate tactics at sea and commando warfare on land. He was brave, intelligent and responsible, and it was not long before he emerged as the buccaneers' natural leader.

At the time Morgan became commander-in-chief of the buccaneer forces in Jamaica, England was actually at war with Spain. This meant that he and his men were privateers, not pirates, and had the official backing of the government for what they did.

Henry Morgan, who was now thirty-three, took advantage of

this situation to embark on the biggest and boldest campaign the buccaneers had ever launched. First he successfully raided several towns in Cuba and Venezuela, and then – in a masterly raid that was to win him great fame and fortune – he turned his attention to the city of Panama, the capital and principal treasure port of the Spanish empire in America. Not even Drake had dared so much.

For the attack on Panama, Morgan assembled the largest force ever seen in those waters – thirty-seven ships with nearly 2,000 English and French buccaneers on board, all first-class fighting men and sworn enemies of the Spanish. Not that the ships would be much use, though, for the buccaneers were on the Caribbean side of the isthmus of Panama and their target was on the Pacific side. Today they could have sailed through the Panama Canal but in Morgan's time they had no alternative but to disembark from the ships and cross the isthmus on foot.

Morgan's first task, then, was to find somewhere safe to leave the ships. The obvious place was the mouth of the River Chagres but this was surprisingly well guarded by the Spanish garrison of Fort San Lorenzo and Morgan had to resort to a direct attack from the landward side. The vanguard charged the fortress with muskets and hand grenades but they had no cover and were forced to retreat under heavy fire, leaving many of their comrades dead below the palisades. 'Why don't the rest of you come and try, you English swine,' the Spaniards shouted after them. 'We'll never let you get to Panama!'

Later in the afternoon a lucky accident gave the buccaneers the chance they had been looking for. One of them happened to be hit in the shoulder by an arrow. This made him so angry that he wrenched it out, wrapped some cotton round the point, set fire to it, stuck the arrow in his musket and fired it into the palm-leaf thatch of some houses inside the fortress walls. His comrades followed suit and several houses were burning fiercely before the Spaniards noticed. Then a roof collapsed on to a barrel of gunpowder. There was a terrific explosion and in the resulting confusion the buccaneers charged again.

Morgan's men laying siege to Fort San Lorenzo.

By now half the fort was on fire but the Spaniards fought like demons. All night the fighting went on: the buccaneers crept through the flames on their hands and knees, sniping at any Spaniards they could see. By dawn the palisades were burnt down. By midday there were only thirty Spaniards left out of more than 300, and most of these were wounded. When they ran out of ammunition they hurled stones at the buccaneers, and when they ran out of stones they jumped to their deaths off the walls rather than surrender.

The resistance was so fierce that by the time it was all over the buccaneers had lost 100 men and sixty were wounded. Afterwards Morgan learnt that it was one of his own men, an Irish deserter, who had warned the Spaniards about the attack. That was why Chagres was so heavily defended, he was told, and why a large Spanish army was already waiting for him outside the gates of Panama City.

A contemporary map of the isthmus and town of Panama.

Undeterred, Morgan set off at the head of his men to cross the isthmus. His route was roughly along the line followed by the Panama Canal today – up the River Chagres, on the Caribbean side of the mountains, in a flotilla of canoes, then down the main mule track on foot to Panama on the Pacific side.

It was very tough country indeed. The mountains were covered in dense rain forest and cut by torrential rivers. The air was hot and sticky and thick, day and night, with swarms of biting insects. The main problem was getting enough to eat for such a large body of men. Morgan had reckoned to live off the land and so had not taken any supplies with him. This was a bad mistake. The rain forest provided no food at all and the deserted army posts and Indian villages they came across were quite empty. After a few days the men were so faint with hunger that they started to eat grass, leaves and even their leather ammunition pouches. (Leather is edible if you know how to cook it right. The buccaneers beat it between two stones, soaked it in water, scraped off the hair, roasted it over some hot embers, cut it up into small pieces and then swallowed the pieces whole.)

After a week's travelling they reached the limits of navigation on the Chagres River. They abandoned their canoes and proceeded on foot in the pouring tropical rain, running a gauntlet of Spanish patrols and Indian ambushes, until they reached the top of the mountains and could see below them the broad blue expanse of the Pacific Ocean and the roofs and spires of Panama. Their spirits rose at the sight and they gave three cheers and threw their hats – more than a thousand of them – into the air. Their spirits rose even further when they saw the large herds of cattle grazing down on the plain. Immediately the buccaneers broke ranks, charged down the mountainside and shot every cow they could get in range of. They were so ravenous that they ate the meat almost raw. The blood trickled down their beards and over their bellies and they were soon blissfully full.

That evening as they were camping on the plain a squadron of Spanish cavalry galloped up and yelled: '*Mañana, Mañana, perros, nos veremos!*' ('Tomorrow, tomorrow, dogs, we'll see what happens!') But the buccaneers were very cool. They didn't take any notice. They just went around collecting hay for their palliases, and after a good night's sleep they marched on Panama.

They marched forward in battle order with drums beating and flags flying. They found the Spanish army already drawn up – two cavalry squadrons of 600 men, four infantry regiments of over 2,000 men, and a secret weapon in the form of a thousand wild bulls driven along by a party of 600 Indians. The buccaneers saw that they were hopelessly outnumbered, but it was out of the question to retreat or surrender so they resolved to press on and fight to the last man. They extended their line in three battalions and advanced behind a forward unit of 200 marksmen. This was the beginning of the first pitched battle between white armies ever fought on American soil.

As soon as the buccaneers were within range the entire Spanish army raised a terrific shout of '*Viva el Rey!*' ('Long live the King!'), and the cavalry went into the attack. But the Spanish commander, Don Guzman, had made a fatal mistake. He had chosen the wrong place to fight. The horses were bogged down in swampy ground before they could reach the buccaneers and Morgan's forward unit were able to pick off

the riders wholesale with their devastatingly accurate and continuous fire. At the same time the Spanish infantry was held in check by the main body of the buccaneers. At this juncture Don Guzman threw in his secret weapon.

The Spanish commander's plan was to drive his bulls into the rear of the buccaneer force and scatter them far and wide in hopeless confusion. But wild bulls are not amenable to discipline. All that the buccaneers had to do was turn round, wave a few flags and fire a few shots in the air and the bulls turned round and charged straight back into the close-packed ranks of the Spanish infantry. With that Don Guzman had lost the battle.

After two hours hard fighting 600 Spanish soldiers lay dead on the battlefield and the rest had fled. The buccaneers stormed the city and after some savage street fighting they captured it. Almost immediately fire broke out in several quarters and spread rapidly. By midnight most of the city – the finest city in America, with many splendid cedarwood buildings – was a

Don Guzman's cavalry foundering in the swampy ground.

Below: Panama in flames and the artist's representation of the battle.

Deſe æthiete ſien op fol: 151

mass of flames. By dawn the capital of the Spanish American empire was in ashes.

Morgan blamed Don Guzman for the outrage. Don Guzman blamed Morgan. Either way it had done nobody any good.

During the three weeks they were in Panama, the buccaneers plundered the entire region by land and sea. But they still got out of hand and committed some terrible atrocities against the Spanish civilians in the area. They tortured them to make them tell where their valuables were hidden – a favourite method was to tighten a cord round a man's skull till his eyes bulged out like eggs – and they looted, raped and murdered without mercy.

Some say Morgan had nothing to do with these atrocities, but he was the man in charge so he took the blame. When one of his men published a book about it some years later, Morgan sued him for libel and won £400 damages. But by then the mud had stuck. From that day to this, rightly or wrongly, Morgan has been known as the cruellest cut-throat who ever trod the Spanish Main.

On 24 February 1671, Morgan left the blackened ruins of Panama City with all his men, and 175 mules laden with treasure, and 500 prisoners for ransom. When he got back to his ships he gave his men the slip and sailed away with most of the treasure in his own possession. With this fortune he bought large estates in Jamaica and settled down as a respectable planter. And for his services the government eventually knighted him and appointed him Deputy Governor of Jamaica. The rest of his life he devoted to the extermination of his old buccaneer comrades, whom he described as 'ravenous vermin'. In 1688 he died of drink, aged fifty-four, fat, rich and famous, a legend to the present day.

In his three years of buccaneering, between 1669 and 1671, Sir Henry Morgan is thought to have acquired 950,000 pieces of eight and a vast quantity of silver plate, jewels, silks, gold and silver lace and other valuables. By today's values this made him a multi-millionaire – and the most successful thief in history.

William Dampier – pirate and circumnavigator.

One day in March 1680 a force of nearly 400 English buccaneers landed on the isthmus to attack Panama a second time. They were under the command of some of Morgan's former lieutenants and included two young men who were later to become famous as explorers and authors – Dr Lionel Wafer, ship's surgeon, and William Dampier, ship's artist (or navigator). William Dampier, who crops up several times in this story, was twenty-eight at the time and as yet unknown. But he was to prove one of the most remarkable of all the buccaneers, and a competent explorer as well. He had a great talent as a navigator, naturalist and writer, and eventually made three voyages round the world – one of them as the official leader of the first English expedition ever to explore the coast of Australia. Fame and fortune, however, were still some way in the future when he set off with Dr Wafer and their dubious companions on this latest raid on the Spanish American capital.

Nearly ten years had passed since Morgan's capture of Panama and the Spaniards had built a fine new city to replace the one he had burnt down. Once more it was the biggest gold and silver port in the world and the buccaneers hoped to find another fortune there. But though they captured five Spanish warships in the harbour, their attack failed, for Panama was now very heavily defended. Naturally the buccaneers were extremely upset by this failure and after a lot of argument some of them decided to give up and go home.

Overleaf: Bartholomew Sharp and some of his men landing on the Galapagos Islands.

The remainder, under the command of Captain Bartholomew Sharp, fancied they might find a fortune in some passing
ship or some Spanish town along the Pacific coast of Spanish
America. So without more ado they unfurled the sails of the
ships they had captured off Panama, and nosed their way out
into the South Seas – the first foreign force to sail there since
Drake.

The voyage of Captain Sharp and his men into the Pacific
Ocean was one of the great feats of seamanship of the age. He
was sailing in virtually unknown waters down an entirely
enemy coast. He had no supplies, no medicines, no charts, and
no clear idea of where he was going. Against sudden squalls
and hidden rocks and all the dangers of the unknown he could
offer nothing but his seaman's skill and instinct.

His first port of call was the Galapagos Islands, where he
took aboard fresh water to drink and giant turtles to eat at sea.
Then he set course down the coast of Peru in search of Spanish
ships and Spanish treasure.

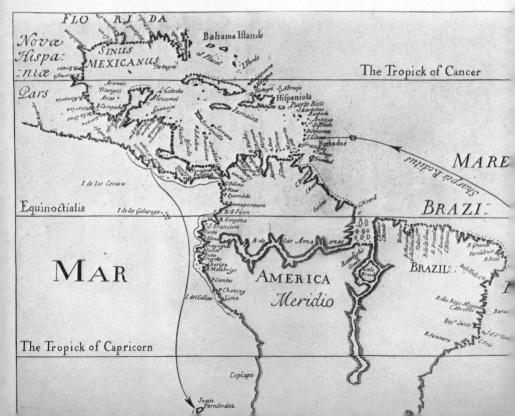

The Spaniards, however, soon got wind of his arrival. As soon as his sails appeared over the horizon the people of the towns hid all their valuables and ran away into the interior. The Spanish cavalry galloped after the raiders as soon as they set foot on shore and demolition experts swam out to their ships on inflated horse hides and tried to set fire to them. The buccaneers began to feel very unwelcome. They couldn't find any loot; some of their friends had been killed in skirmishes with the army; and now the rest of them were beginning to go down with scurvy, a common disease on ships in those days, when no fruit or vegetables were available.

They decided to spend Christmas on a lonely and unin-habited little island called Juan Fernandez. They all agreed it was the worst Christmas they had spent for a long time. They drank what was left of the wine, fired their guns into the air to cheer themselves up, then started to grumble and gamble and fight each other for the few pieces of eight they had left. When they set sail they were near to mutiny and in the confusion left an American Indian member of their crew behind by mistake. By the time another ship picked him up four years later, in 1684, he had been on his own so long that he had lost the power of human speech.

The buccaneers cruised about with no better luck and even-tually forty-seven of them – including William Dampier and Dr Wafer – mutinied and set off home in two canoes. Of the original force of 400 men there were now only seventy-five left, all in one ship.

After the mutiny their luck changed. First they captured a Spanish cargo ship with 37,000 pieces of eight on board. Then they captured another with a hold full of treasure, together with 620 jars of brandy and the most beautiful woman any of them had ever seen in the South Seas. After looting the ship they let it go with the beautiful woman still on board. Then they decided to go home at last and set the course to the South-wards. This was the start of one of the most brilliant voyages in sailing history.

Their plan was to return to the Caribbean via Cape Horn

27

Bartholomew Sharp's incredible voyage.

and the Atlantic. Not even Drake had sailed that far south and no Englishmen had ever rounded the Horn before. But Sharp and his men had no alternative. For weeks they drove through mountainous seas and howling gales. Then in early November they lost sight of land in thick fog and for the next three months navigated an unknown ocean without the help of any landmarks. But they rounded the Horn safely and Christmas Day found them off the coast of Brazil. Captain Sharp noted in his log book:

We eat our hogg and drank severall jarrs of wine and was extraordinary merry, whome god preserve and send us in safety to our desired port.

Sure enough, with wonderful accuracy, they eventually reached their desired port of Barbados in January 1682 after a return journey of 10,000 miles. They had been away three years. These buccaneers had proved themselves the greatest seamen of their age, and when Captain Sharp published his book about their venture into the South Seas it roused the interest of the world and paved the way for the future exploration of the Pacific by Captain Cook and others.

Rounding the Horn.

But what had happened to the forty-seven men who had mutinied and left Captain Sharp in April 1681?

They managed to reach the isthmus of Panama in their two canoes and most of them struggled across to the other side where they were rescued by a friendly ship lying off-shore. At least two of their company were not so lucky. One, weighed down by a satchel full of silver dollars, stumbled and drowned when he was crossing a stream. Another, injured in an accident, was left behind in the jungle to die. He was none other than Dr Wafer, the buccaneers' surgeon.

One evening during the march through the forest, one of Dr Wafer's companions decided to dry out his damp gunpowder by heating it on a silver plate held over the campfire. This was a dangerous thing to do. There was a very big explosion and poor Dr Wafer, who was sitting nearby, caught the full force of the blast: his thigh was burnt and his knee torn open to the bone. In the middle of an unexplored forest, and miles from help, the doctor suddenly found himself a helpless cripple.

Originally the buccaneers had agreed to kill anybody who lagged behind, but they hadn't the heart to shoot their doctor and for five days he hobbled behind them through the trees. Then one night a slave ran off with the medicine chest and Dr Wafer became so depressed that he asked to be left behind. His only chance, he thought, was to throw himself on the mercy of the Indians.

Dr Wafer was a brave and clever man. Though his wound was turning gangrenous and causing him great pain, he didn't panic when the last of his friends waved goodbye to him. Instead, he found his way to a village inhabited by a tribe of wild Indians, and there he stayed for four extraordinary months.

At first the Indians gave him a hard time. The young warriors wanted to sacrifice him. They made him beg like a dog for scraps of food and took it in turns to kick him. But oddly enough they went to great pains to treat his wound and Dr Wafer was astonished how effective their remedies were. First they collected some special herbs and plants from the forest, then they chewed them into a paste, spread the paste over the wound and covered it with a banana leaf as a bandage. The primitive Indian's medicine was better than the white man's, and in three weeks Dr Wafer was completely cured.

At length the Indians allowed the doctor to leave their village to try and catch up with his companions. But there were no paths in the forest and he was soon hopelessly lost. He was filthy, and ragged, and dizzy with hunger and exhaustion when he stumbled into a second Indian village. Once again the Indians saved the English doctor's life.

This time they were much more friendly. They fed him and gave him a hut and a hammock to sleep in. They stripped off his tattered old clothes, examined his strange white skin with great curiosity, then painted his naked body from head to foot with pictures of yellow birds and purple flowers. Finally they hung a golden ornament like a cockle shell from his nose. Thus attired, Dr Wafer spent the next few months living like an Indian. He hunted with them, ate with them, slept with them, learned their language and studied their ways. In the end he grew very fond of them. They were tall, beautiful and athletic. They were gentle to each other, considerate to their women and kind to their children. They liked the doctor a lot. In fact they liked him so much that he began to think they would never let him go. The chief only allowed him to leave on condition that he would return and marry his daughter and bring back a pack of English hounds for hunting. (But he never did.)

After a difficult crossing of the mountains, Dr Wafer at last reached the Caribbean coast, and there by happy chance lay a buccaneer sailing ship with all his old shipmates on board. The doctor immediately put out in a canoe and climbed on deck. He was still painted yellow and purple like an Indian and he still wore a gold cockle shell in his nose, so it was an hour before his friends saw through the disguise. Then one of them, peering closely at him as he squatted Indian-fashion by the ship's rails, suddenly cried out: 'Here's our doctor!' and immediately he was surrounded by well-wishers congratulating him on his safe return and laughing at his bizarre appearance.

So ended the adventures of Dr Lionel Wafer, surgeon, among

the wild Indians of Panama. It was a unique experience and he later wrote a book about it which contained a valuable picture of Indian tribal life in the seventeenth century.

By the time Lionel Wafer returned from his stay among the Indians in 1681, the Caribbean had already become an uncomfortable place for buccaneers. In the previous year the English Government, realizing it was now becoming more profitable to trade with the Spaniards than attack them and rob them had decided to crack down on buccaneering. A squadron of naval warships was sent to the West Indies to winkle the buccaneers out of their old haunts, and one day a navy frigate sailed into Port Royal with four of them hanging from the yard arms. Everyone then knew that the game was up.

Some buccaneers vanished into the empty spaces of the Pacific. Others ended their days in hiding among the Panama Indians. Some became ordinary pirates. A few, like William Dampier and Ambrose Cowley, left the scene of their crimes altogether, sailed round the world, wrote books and became famous. Others, who had managed to save some money, became respectable planters, and one actually took Holy Orders and rose to be Archbishop of York – though he could never quite abandon his old habits and used to keep his brandy bottles in the pulpit and his girl friends in the vestry.

As for Dr Wafer, he made a second buccaneering foray into the Pacific after his adventures with the Indians. When he got back in 1688 he made straight for Virginia, hoping that nobody there would ask him any questions. But he was caught red-handed in a tiny rowing boat full of loot as he tried to slip ashore with a couple of shipmates and spent the next year or two in and out of an American prison.

Eventually Dr Wafer and his two shipmates were set free and most of their swag was returned to them. But by the time the doctor reached England in 1690 buccaneering had become part of history. A year or two later the last vestiges of it disappeared for ever when the buccaneer base at Port Royal in Jamaica suddenly vanished from the face of the earth.

33

Dr Wafer rescued by the Indians.

Some of the treasure recovered from the drowned Port Royal.

The destruction of Port Royal and most of its inhabitants was so swift and terrible that many people thought it was God's punishment for their wicked ways. Just before lunchtime on 7 June 1692 the ground began to heave and tremble and whole houses, whole streets even, sank into the earth. Screaming people rushed into the streets and then slid helplessly into great cracks, which slowly closed and crushed them. After the earthquake had died down a huge tidal wave swept over the town. It smashed a fortress to pieces; it drove a navy ship into the centre of town, where it came to rest on the top of some houses; it broke open the cemetery and washed the bodies out into the streets. Several thousand people died and many more were injured or made homeless in the catastrophe. Port Royal still lies at the bottom of the sea, and from time to time underwater archaeologists bring up from the drowned taverns and buried houses the bones and rum bottles and pieces of eight of the buccaneers who had once frequented them.

Ten years after Port Royal had slipped into the sea, England and Spain were once again at war. But this time the English Government was determined to put seaborne operations against the Spanish on a more official basis than the buccaneer activities had ever been. Naval squadrons already stationed in the Caribbean were strengthened. And for more extensive raids into the Pacific proper privateer expeditions were fitted out and manned in English ports.

The great ambition of most of these privateer expeditions was to capture one of the fabulous Spanish galleons that sailed each year from Manila in the Philippines to Acapulco in Mexico laden with all the silks and spices and precious stuff of the East. The Manila galleons were reputed to be the biggest, strongest and most splendid ships in the world and each one of them carried cargoes worth up to 14,000,000 pieces of eight. One of them had been captured more than a hundred years previously by an Elizabethan sea captain called Thomas Cavendish. Since then they had eluded everyone. The buccaneers had tried; William Dampier had tried in 1704; four years later it was Woodes Rogers turn.

The privateer expedition commanded by Captain Woodes Rogers consisted of two ships – the *Duke*, 320 tons, thirty guns, and the *Duchess*, 260 tons, twenty-six guns – which had been fitted out by a group of Bristol merchants at a cost of £13,000.

35

Overleaf: The destruction of Port Royal.

A sea battle.

The two ships were legal men-of-war and Captain Rogers was determined to keep Navy-style discipline on board them. He had double the usual number of officers – including William Dampier, who signed on as pilot for what was to be his third and final voyage round the world – and kept a firm hand on the men throughout the cruise. A lot of these men were land-lubbers recruited in Ireland as a reserve crew in case sickness at sea depleted the regular crews.

During the last months of 1708 the two ships sailed steadily southwards into warmer waters. When they crossed the Tropic of Cancer they celebrated the event by ducking every member of the crew who had never crossed the tropic before. Many of the crew, in fact, had never even been to sea before, so to them the celebrations must have seemed even more terrifying. One by one, former tinkers, haymakers, peddlars and fiddlers were hoisted half way up to the yard-arm by a rope round their feet and there they dangled for a brief moment before the other end of the rope was let go and the novice sailors hurtled headfirst into the ocean. Captain Rogers thought this custom was a good thing. The men needed a wash, he said.

Early in January 1709 the ships rounded the Horn into the Pacific and set course for the old uninhabited buccaneer island of Juan Fernandez. When they arrived they were surprised to see a strange light on the shore and the next day Woodes Rogers sent a boat to investigate and take on water: 'Immediately our pinnace returned from the shore with a man clothed in goatskins who looked wilder than the first owners of them. He had been on the island four years and four months. His name was Alexander Selkirk, Scotch man' – the man who was to become world famous in his own lifetime as the original model for the story of *Robinson Crusoe*. Selkirk, a Scot, had been mate on a ship that had called at Juan Fernandez earlier and had been marooned on the island at his own request because of a quarrel with his captain. He had apparently remained fit and cheerful for the whole of that time living in a grass hut full of cats and eating mainly wild goats and crawfish. He had passed the time by reading, singing and praying. Captain Rogers had no hesitation in appointing him to the rank of mate on his own ship, the *Duke*, before continuing the voyage to the northwards.

After an attack on the port of Guayaquil, the expedition made for the Bay of Panama and took stock of their takings so far. These amounted to £20,000 in gold, silver and jewels, £60,000 in merchandise, three ships, 100 slaves for future sale and 180 prisoners for future ransom. From the privateers' point of view it was becoming a lucrative little cruise. But the best was yet to come, for the time was drawing near when the Manila galleon would make its landfall after the long voyage from the Philippines.

The Manila galleon was not an easy ship to intercept. There was no sure way of knowing exactly where it would turn up, but William Dampier had advised Captain Rogers that Cape St Lucas, California, was a likely spot and by the end of October the three biggest ships – the *Duke*, the *Duchess*, and a

Overleaf: The rescue of Alexander Selkirk – Robinson Crusoe.

captured one renamed the *Marquis* – were at action stations off the Californian coast. The ships were spread out along a forty-five mile line, each ship just in sight of its neighbour. That way they covered as much as they could of the area where the galleon was expected to arrive.

For three weeks they waited but not a sail did they see and when they began to run out of food and water they reluctantly decided they could wait no longer. No sooner had they put in for water, however, than the lookout at the masthead cried out that he saw a strange sail about seven leagues distance. It was the Manila galleon after all.

The English ships put out after her and by dawn on 22 December the *Duke* was about three miles astern of the galleon and the *Duchess* about two miles ahead of her. There was great excitement on board all three ships. Captain Rogers ordered hot chocolate for his crew, then said prayers, but as he did so the galleon opened up with all her guns. At that he drew up the *Duke* alongside her and gave her several broadsides and raked her from the bows, while the *Duchess* did the same. There was absolute silence from the galleon. Then she lowered her flag in surrender.

Only two Englishmen had been wounded and it was unfortunate that Captain Rogers was one of them. A bullet had struck him in the left cheek and shattered his upper jaw, part of which fell on the deck where he stood. It was a bad wound and it prevented him from talking, so from then on he had to put his orders in writing. Even so he had no intention of leaving the scene. The galleon he had captured was richly laden, but Rogers learnt that it was only the first and smallest of two galleons that had sailed from Manila that year. A bigger and richer prize was due to arrive at any moment.

Sure enough, on Christmas Day 1709, the great ship hove into view. She was a giant of a ship, 900 tons, with a crew of 450 men and sixty big guns – a formidable proposition for Rogers's small craft. Nevertheless, the *Duchess* and the *Marquis* closed on her at once and the *Duke* crowded on sail to catch up. For that day and the next the English ships fought a running action with the Spanish ship. But it was no use. The English cannon balls just bounced off the stout teak sides of the Spanish galleon, while the Spanish cannon balls went straight through the frailer oak sides of the English vessels. Woodes Rogers was wounded yet again, this time in the heel, and at last agreed to call the whole thing off. The disappointed privateers watched the galleon pull away and vanish over the horizon. Then they set sail for home via the Cape of Good Hope.

It had been one of the most successful expeditions of all. In England the haul was eventually sold for £150,000 (worth well over a million pounds today) and the officers and crew received a substantial share. William Dampier retired from the sea. As for Woodes Rogers, he recovered from his wounds, grew rich, and in 1717 was appointed Captain-General and Governor-in-Chief of the Bahama Islands with the special duty of stamping out piracy in the Caribbean – a task he set about as efficiently as he had the capture of the famous Manila galleon.

Woodes Rogers, Governor of the Bahaman Islands, with his family.

The capture of the Manila galleon.

The notorious Blackbeard (Capt. John Teach).

By the time Woodes Rogers reached the Bahamas, piracy had been flourishing in those waters for many years. The pirates were men of all nations and preyed upon ships of all nations. They owed allegiance to nobody, obeyed no rules, and knew no home. The secret coves and anchorages of the Bahamas were their favourite hideouts, Madagascar was their favourite base, and the Red Sea and the Persian Gulf were their favourite hunting grounds. They ranged the world on what was called the pirate round. Now, rather than looking for Spanish ships they went after Indian ones, and for preference they sold their ill-gotten loot in the American colonies rather than in Europe. Some of the most extraordinary pirates of those days are still famous today – men like the ferocious Captain Teach (*alias* Blackbeard) who was reputedly married fourteen times, or Captain Kidd, the respectable pirate hunter who turned pirate himself and was eventually hung in chains in London, or the two extraordinary lady pirates, Anne Bonney and Mary Read, who both served on the same pirates ship disguised as men, though neither knew the other was a woman.

But the story of these notorious villains is not really the story of the Spanish Main at all, for they did most of their swashbuckling in different seas, and since they were a menace to all civilized nations they were soon stamped out. By 1720 the golden age of piracy was over – a source of legend and romance to the present day.

In 1716, the ferocious Blackbeard (Capt. John Teach) was finally killed by Lieutenant Maynard of the Royal Navy after a desperate hand-to-hand battle on board Teach's ship, the Revenge. *Blackbeard finally fell wounded by five pistol balls and twenty cuts and stabs, and Lieutenant Maynard sailed the* Revenge *into the city of Charleston, her prow adorned with Teach's severed head.*

Index